Helen Francesca Bantock

The Love-Philtre

And other Poems

Helen Francesca Bantock

The Love-Philtre
And other Poems

ISBN/EAN: 9783337401313

Printed in Europe, USA, Canada, Australia, Japan

Cover: Foto ©Andreas Hilbeck / pixelio.de

More available books at **www.hansebooks.com**

THE LOVE-PHILTRE AND OTHER POEMS

HELEN F. SCHWEITZER

LONDON

John Macqueen

1897

CONTENTS

	PAGE
THE LOVE-PHILTRE, . .	I
THE WANDERER, . . .	18
WHISPERS OF SPRING, .	21
AN APRIL DAY, .	23
SPRING YEARNING,	25
MY LOST JUNE, .	27
THE LOVE ANGEL, .	31
PAUSE,	40
LOVE'S SACRAMENT,	41
THE HEDONIST, .	42
IRREVOCABLE, . .	43
LINES,	50

vii

CONTENTS

A MOONLESS NIGHT,

MEMORY'S LYRE, .

DO I LOVE THEE ?

LIFE,

RAIN,

LIMITATIONS, .

SONG,

MAY, .

NOW !

AN ARABIAN LOVE SONG,

AVE ATQUE VALE, .

THE LOVE PHILTRE

So Tristram took the sea with fair Ysolt—

Ysolt the beautiful, Mark's destined bride—

And thro' the long, blue summer days they sailed

Ever away. In some unbroken dream

They lingered, while sweet sleeping Love laid still,

His singing silent, and his down-drooped brow

Rosy with shadow of the plumes which tipped

His pinions. Fragrant as the dewy heart

Of some deep rose, which in full summer blooms,

A

In the warm darkness with wideshielding wings,

Fold upon fold about him, there he lay,

So lightly sleeping, that the happy sighs

Which broke from those two watching lovers stirred

His slumber, and a shaft of quiv'ring fire

Stole from the hidden splendour of his gaze.

But Fate's full hour dawned not, nor yet had Time

Run out his falling sands, when Love should spring

Dominant, splendid, strong, with eyes like flame

To burn the body's veil, and to disclose

His image mirrored true within their souls.

Truth is Love's seal, set on the lips and brow

And o'er the spirit's pure unclouded glass,

To guard his image there.   Once broken through,

Love knows his face no more, for the world creeps

To gaze, and with a thousand gaudy shows

Troubles the clear reflection.   Love alone

With Truth can dwell ; from falsity he flies.

So they sailed on ; but every heart-beat drew

Them nearer to that fate-appointed hour.

This wise it came :

                              The long and golden spell

Of summer sunlight sudden turned to grey.

And one still eve the low, long storm-lines crept

On drear horizons, save where, in the west,

The lurid sunset burned with smouldering fire.

Becalmed their vessel lay.   An oily sleep

Sent its slow undulations o'er the sea,

And a hot wind, with fitful angers, flapped

The listless sails.   A heavy languor drew

The blood from Ysolt's cheek, leaving it wan

Beneath the shadow of her clouding hair.

But one red, sunset gleam stole where she lay,

And, like Love's rosiest plume, upon her breast

Lingered in crimson glow.   No colour else

About her.   White her clinging gown, and pearls,

Drawn by her father's divers from deep seas,

THE LOVE PHILTRE

Circled her throat's warm snow.   Only that shaft

Of crimson burned ; and Tristram, entering

The cabin, marked it with a curious thrill

Thro' every vein.

                Ah ! seemed she not like snow,

This fair Ysolt—snow unapproachable

On highest mountain brows—she, destined queen

Of all Mark's lordly realm.   Yet, yon bold ray

Slept there upon her heart ! and Love might steal

Within.

                So love and knightly honour strove

For mastery.   His promise to the king

Of bride, the noblest and the fairest maid

Of Ireland ; and his own rebellious blood,

Which fain would break all barriers to burn

In one long kiss upon her lips, then flow

In death's dark stream, washing that stain away.

So long he silent mused, that, wondering,

She called him, and soft broke his troubled dream

With her low voice's music.

                   ' Grace, fair maid,

And pardon, sith my mood to-day hath ta'en

The day's grey colour.' So he sighed and stepped

Beside her, and in listless reverie,

Plucking her couch's silken fringes, drew

A sudden sound from his own harp which lay

There hidden.   Part in pain, part irony,

 Brave harp,' he cried, ' muffled in silken thrall,

Thou play'st but muted melody.   Like harp,

My heart—wild heart of Tristram, caught and dumb

With winding Love, and manhood drained away

By dallying weakness.   Oh ! for one clear strain

Of woodland music, when the harp strings sang

To all the winds of heaven, and when my heart was

    free.'

Swiftly he swept the lyre, till loud and wild

The echoes rang, and all the listening soul

In Ysolt's brooding eyes leapt to his song.

' Ah ! boldly blow, my silver-sounding horn,

Swiftly awake the echoes of the morn ;

Now sounding strong, now keen, and sweet and clear.

The waiting woods thy winding music hear,

Sending the sudden lark to cleave the blue,

Startling the fawn from sleep in fern and dew

To brush the deep green coverts, and to fly

Before that note of warning minstrelsy.

Then, ere the sun has pierced the shrouding grey,

Swift to the chase, my merry men, away !

Ah ! swiftly wake, sweet echoes of the morn,

Ride, ride and blow the silver-sounding horn.'

He paused, with bold blue eyes aflame, and laughed

THE LOVE PHILTRE

To hear the echoes ring, and dashed the chords

Again, till Ysolt, fired by Tristram's mood

And fancy, trilled, in laughing mimicry,

The echo strains, then fain would strike and play

Her lessoned notes, learned in those sweet past hours

When her sure skill had healed him of his wound,

Yet pierced him with a soul-wound deeper still.

Then happed it they were thirsty, and they saw

A golden goblet stand, filled with red wine.

Crusted with gems the cup, and, lo ! a snake,

With gleaming length, was coiled about its stem.

Relentless as that close embrace, Love held

The hearts of those who drank of that love-wine

Within his deathless pow'r. Upon the brim,

Engraved by some quaint carver's skill, two hearts

Were close entwined, while grim and baffled Death

Thrust cruel darts in vain ; the life blood flowed,

And mingling in its flow, sprang up in fire,

A bright and deathless flame for evermore.

Now, when the queen, her mother, bade farewell

To Ysolt, to her maid, and Gouvernail,

Tristram's chief squire, she had this love-drink giv'n,

And charged them, on that day, when Mark, the king,

Should wed her daughter, that day they should give

To him this draught to drink unto his bride,

So that a deathless love within their hearts

Should dwell forever.

               Tristram, wondering

At those strange things enwrought thereon, took up

The goblet. 'Surely with right noble wine

Our man and maid thought to have kept good cheer.'

Bright with the blood of sun-warmed grape the tide

Flowed free.

           'To thee, thou fairest queen, to thee

I drink !   Ysolt, one draught to me drink thou !'

She took the cup, and drained it.   Then their eyes

THE LOVE PHILTRE

Met in one startled, long, bewildering gaze.

Breathless they stood ; while in each throbbing breast

A flame leapt up, burning their souls laid bare ;

And in the silence, as of coming doom,

They heard the sighing wind.   Fear was about them.

Ghostly shadows crept, while still the rising flame

Shuddered within.   Sudden to one embrace

They sprang, while earth, and sea, and sky whirled, slipped,

And rushed away—they, only they alone

In all the universe, ringed round with fire—

With fire above, below, around, within.

Then from her hand the cup, with heavy clang,

Clashed to the ground, and the world rolled again

Between them, hurrying a rose-red glow

To Ysolt's cheek, while Tristram slowly bent

To raise the cup, kissing her garment's hem ;

But Ysolt caught away the gown, and sank,

Till all her whiteness clung upon his breast

Like snow wind-driven.

                 ' Ah ! my mountain snow

At last,' he cried, ' seen, yearned for, kissed and won.'

And she, half-sobbing, murmured—' Tristram, thine !—

Thine, though thy brightness should consume away

The snow in fire—ay, in a mist of flame !

Yet, would I die thus, faint, and fade and fail,

Lost in thy light, my sun, my soul's desire.

But in a drifting cloud I would arise

To kiss thy face, to crown thy brow, to cling

Closely about thee.   When the day was done,

Upon my bosom thou should'st gently sink,

Thy weary splendour flooding all my soul

With crimson glory.   Through the night's still gloom

I would drop dews upon thee till the dawn ;

Then, like mist-wreaths before the morning glow,

I'd float away, drawn up, dissolved in thee—

Part of thy life forever.   Tristram, thou

Whom in my dreams I saw, ere from the dim

Blue line of sea thy sail appeared and grew

White-winged upon the plunging grey-green wave ;

Till, lo ! one eve, when March's clarion wind

Blew from red skies, they brought thee to our hall,

A wounded lion with a tawny mane,

Stiff with the salt sea brine, and dark with foam.

And when the wild rough warriors of the west—

My father's knights of Ireland—clustered round

To question thee, thy hands caught up thy harp

And swept the strings until the rafters rang.

And the fierce hearts around throbbed with fierce glee

At the wild music of that joyous strain.

Ah ! never knight harped thus in that dark isle,

Ringed with the moaning winds, and sad with sound

And long-drawn thunder of the restless sea.

Then to my care, the king, my father, gave thee.

I healed thee of thy dolorous wound ; but thou,

Winding thy music round my heart-strings, drew

Love's music from them, and I loved but thee.

When thou wert strong, and wandered far afield

In mighty huntings, lonely would I sit,

And lean my cheek upon thy harp, and kiss

The strings thy hands had touched ; then, half-afraid,

Half-angry, I would fret against the pow r

Which bound me, flinging thee in scorn light jests

And hiding, with a veil of cold, white calm,

My wild heart's fire.   But thou hast pierced the snow,

And found the fire.   Tristram, my sun, my king,

I love thee !   I am thine, and mine art thou ! '

Then, with a cry, he kissed her once again.

Thus worked the charm, and drew their hearts in one,

Ere ever Ysolt to Mark's kingdom came.

B

THE WANDERER

DEEP down in my heart a wee floweret grew,

And a little brown songbird was nestling there, too ;

And all through the winter, the mist and the snow,

They laid there together and heard the winds blow.

Oh ! wanderer, roaming from out the far West,

Leave them still in their darkness, and silence and rest !

When the year was yet young, and the wild wind of March

Powdered snow on the thorn, and green tasselled the larch,

Love and Spring wandered by, and the flower-bud stirred

Beneath the soft breast of the little brown bird.

Oh! Wanderer, roaming from out the far West,

Leave them still in their darkness, and silence and rest!

But the shadows grew greener deep down in the wood,

Love and Spring strayed together in sweet solitude ;

All the air was a fragrance, the earth was a bower,

And the bird woke to song, and the bud to a flower ;

And the Wanderer, roaming from out the far West,

Took the bird to his heart, bore the flower on his breast.

Then the flower bloomed sweetly the whole summer long,

And the bird filled all heaven with rapturous song ;

And when Winter came near, and the trees turned to brown,

And the last leaves of Autumn came fluttering down,

Then the Wanderer, roaming from out the far West,

Still sheltered them both in the warmth of his breast.

And he covered them up with a soft cloud of blue,

With silence and sweetness, with darkness and dew ;

And a heart which was lonely he took for his home,

For, weary of wandering, no more will he roam.

And Love overshadowed them all with his wing

While they dreamed there together, to wake with next Spring !

WHISPERS OF SPRING

Hush! you can hear,

If you bend down your ear.

Though the earth is brown,

And the seed but just sown,

Yet, if you bend down,

You can hear!

Ah! a soft shudder going,

And a sweet life-sap flowing

WHISPERS OF SPRING

Through the tender things growing,

Which full soon will be blowing,

Though, as yet, old Earth's brown,

And the wild heavens frown ;

But only bend down,

    Then you'll hear !

AN APRIL DAY

Love is an April day

    Of grey and golden weather.

Come, shall we go the woodland way,

    Thou, I and Love together?

High on yon blooming spray,

    Trills the first bird of Spring.

But, ah! Love's sweeter lay,

    We happy twain shall sing—

    Love is an April day!

Love is an April day

Of sun and shadow flying ;

To-morrow thou wilt say me nay,

To-day, ah ! no denying.

The wind in some sweet glade,

Flutters the white wind-flower ;

So shall our souls have played

With Love one sun-kissed hour.

Love is an April day !

SPRING YEARNING

On some sweet day of middle-Spring,

When all the fields are blossoming,

When the wide air, with fragrant incense weighed,

Wanders in delicate orchard shade,

And pausing gently, with a wilful breath,

Woos the soft blossom from its opening sheath,

And tender leaflets fluttering for flight.

How sweet it were on such a day, or night

25

Of lovelier enchantment, silently

To sleep and dream, and sleeping, cease to be !

The Spring's soft tumult in the blood,

Like mounting sap within the wood,

In dreams weaves such sweet magic in the brain,

That, waking, we would dream again ;

Or, haply, on some odour float away—

Some breathing, faint, delicious scent of May—

Or, on some throstle's clear, reiterant song,

Which tries its piping all the warm day long,

Till the tranced spirit, out of sheer delight,

Follows the last high note, and swift takes flight !

MY LOST JUNE

I LOOK out o'er the wold.

Twilight is grey and cold,

A mist of rain

Clouds o'er the pane—

Where's June?

My June of rose and dew,

Of leaves sun-filtered through,

27

Near shadowed stream ;

June's but a dream—

This June.

Where is that June, when I,

Breathing 'neath June's own sky,

Drank through my soul

The perfect whole,

All June ?

Yes ! all her pearls of dawn

Dropped down on leaf and lawn,

And each bird's song,

Which doth belong

  To June.

All their sweet notes I heard–

Each music-throated bird—

Which shook and trilled

Till sense o'er-filled

  With tune.

But now my soul in vain

Yearns for those songs again.

The birds seem flown,

The sad winds moan

Too soon.

Only my lone heart stays,

Remembering past days ;

And left behind,

Still seeks to find

My June !

THE LOVE ANGEL

SOMEONE, light singing, 'twixt a smile and sigh,

Sang in the Spring, ' Love is a butterfly ! '

But sudden Summer leapt with thund'rous eves,

Red - gleaming through the gloom of clustered

　　leaves,

And, with a rush of light and flame,

The passionate Love angel came.

With one sweep of his mighty wing,

31

He struck the sweet flowers of the Spring.

Passion-pale his face,

Lightning-swift his eyes,

Piercing eternities.

And the magic of his singing

Filleth every place.

Lo ! beneath his tread

Splendid blossoms red

In every bower up-springing.

Which softly, strangely, through the gloom,

'Thrill every sense with rich perfume.

Drawing within his strong control

The trembling love-bewildered soul,

Which, all so lightly to its lyre,

Sang, ' Love is but a light desire,

A smile, a sigh,

A butterfly ! '

Lo ! the great angel sweeps the strings,

And heavenward lifts his voice and sings.

' Love ' is the song the spheres

Sang in the morning years,

When, high and clear, together

They sang through heaven's blue weather ;

And the angels listened long

To the sweetness of that song.

C

I, too, listened, wonder-thrilled,

All my soul with love o'er-filled,

And a strange, new power springing

To the magic of that singing.

Love around, beneath, above,

All my life, my soul, was love!

Then a voice from the great Throne

Spoke, and spoke to me alone,—

' Thou thy kingdom dost inherit ;

Love the link 'twixt flesh and spirit,

Love thy sceptre, love thy crown,

To the sad earth bear it down.'

On my pinions, swift and strong,

Down I bore the glad, sweet song.

Crowned above each fellow-angel,

Sang the glorious love-evangel,

Sang it over land and sea,

' Love is Immortality.'

Love within the lover's eyes

Bids the soul of hope arise ;

Love returned, or sweetly given,

Lifts the spirit nearer heaven.

Love, the healer of life's pain.

Sweet to love—be loved again !

Sweet, ah ! passing sweet, to stand

Heart to heart, and hand in hand,

Journeying thro' life together,

Thro' its sad or sunny weather,

Thro' its tumult finding rest,

Clinging to one faithful breast.

When my mighty pinions sweep,

Great deep answers unto deep,

Cold hearts burn with living fire

At the sounding of my lyre,

And my songs resistless roll,

Soul revealing unto soul.

In that soul-apocalypse,

Earth grows pale, and swift Time slips

Onward, upward, ever winging

Up to heaven, on my singing ;

In that rush of meeting breath,

Life, too keen, seems nigh to death.

Lips that kiss, and kiss again,

Joy that almost thrills to pain,

Every wild and sweet emotion

Surging over Love's wide ocean,

Sweetest fear, and dear distress,

Broken words of tenderness.

All the wonder of the rose,

From the dull, black earth-clod grows ;

Thro' the farthest star that shineth

Man a mighty Law divineth ;

Nature to perfection blends

Simple means to noble ends.

By the lips is love confessed,

Soul thro' body is expressed ;

Love's sweet passion, thro' us thrilling,

Life's pure mission is fulfilling.

To the highest Truth above

Nature draws us up by love.

To the dweller in Truth's shrine,

Where Love's holy fires shine.

Earthly death and danger hover

O'er the maiden, o'er the lover ;

Love must brave the earthly doom,

Strong to fight and overcome.

As the gold thro' fire is tried,

Love by pain is purified ;

For rarest pearl beneath the wave

His life the dauntless diver gave.

Then plunge beneath the treacherous brine,

Brave death, give life, and love is thine !

PAUSE

Body, the spirit sleeps in thee ; then wakes,

Haply some eve when rain is in the air,

And God seems very silent 'ere He shakes

His sudden thunders, shoots His lightning flare

O'er shuddering earth and soul alike laid bare.

LÒVE'S SACRAMENT

My life was dim until you came

To light it with a purer flame;

Self-bound my soul, until you rent

Its bonds—a kiss the sacrament.

Your life's white angel in its flight

Lifts mine for ever to the light;

Up-bears my failing spirit's wing

With tender overshadowing.

The sweetest woman earth has known

Has called me, crowned me, for her own!

41

THE HEDONIST

Fill me Life's bumper to the brim ;

Give me the cup, I'll drain it down !

I want no Lethe for despair ;

I only want to do and dare

What sages teach, what poets dream,

Within one foaming draught to drown

Life's perfect pearl, then toss it down !

IRREVOCABLE

YES ! put out the candles to hide your eyes—so !

Now, steal from my chamber athwart the red glow

Of the fire burnt low,

And leave me to slumber, and leave me to dreams—

Happy dreams of the poets I read, or the reams

That I write, or so seems.

Alone ! yet the scorn of those eyes haunts me now,

And I still feel the cold of that kiss on my brow ;

Sick fancies, I trow !
43

The cold, did I say ?   Ah ! the touch burns and sears ;

Burns the brow from its rest, and the eyes from their tears,

Not the heart from its fears !

Pure and proud, pure and high, on your delicate face

Grief has lingered, has left there a saddening trace,

Nobly sad, but not base.

Yes, sorrow has pierced you with sure, savage aim,

And regret, too, has burnt out your heart in its flame,

But, ah, God ! never shame !

Snow, whitest when falling, shows earth's touch the more.

Your soul, like stained marble, cleans white as before ;

It is white to the core.

Mine, seemingly colder, melts fast as the snow,

And, frozen in heaven, turns mud down below ;

 The world changes so !

Fling the marble and snow in the waves. Which shall be

Surest plummet to fathom the depths of the sea ?

 A weird easy to dree.

Shape the two, in the image of Love, let us say,

And Love in the snow lasts the length of a day,

 But in marble, for aye.

Oh ! leave me, cold eyes, with your glance clear and keen,

Oh ! leave me, cold lips, with the cold words between,

 Such a calm ' might have been.'

Take those words from my brain, take those clear eyes away,

Both have pierced to my heart, and it is, as you say,

As you see, common clay !

Earth, pleased with the light of a sun or a star ;

A field, when the hoofs of the battle are far,

Green again after war.

Sand, ribbed by the waves, or marked by the fall

Of the footsteps of men, or by creatures that crawl,

Sand, alike to them all.

As changing as ocean, the breeze, or the skies,

Or a pool, heaven reflecting in ripples which rise

With the swirl of the flies.

Common clay, flawed by doubt and discoloured by sin ;

Yet 'tis white as the world counts, and worthy to win.

White without—but within ?

Common clay, do you think it, like gold, is divine ?

If you rub it for ever it never will shine,

Save as glass will refine.

Common clay, ah ! the scorn of it rang in your tone

As you said, 'Neither truth, neither trust you have shown.'

No—I wrestle alone.

Alone, for I'll run not the chance of a thrust

From your scorn-lance, nor fit me to wear your disgust,

As the weak always must.

No, no ; I will turn you the world's outward side,

And the weaknesses hide them as best I may hide ;

I have still left some pride.

Reproach not the heart which would strivingly show

But the best that you think, and the best that you know,

Not its lowness, so low.

Would that heart were as worthy as yours to lay bare.

Ah ! the snow in the fire but hardly would fare,

But the gold shines, how rare !

And forgive then the effort which still makes you deem

I am silent and trustless ; 'tis only to seem

Not more weak than you dream.

Yes, the light is put out, and the embers are cold,

Fallen ashes to ashes, a tale that is told,

And the night's waning old.

D

LINES

TO THOSE WHO PREFER THE PEACE OF STAGNATION
TO THE WAR OF PROGRESS.

PEACE ! do you prate of peace while hearts throb on in pain ?

Peace ! do you prate of peace when a burning scar of Cain

Is branded on innocent brows, through no fault of their own,

Save that the children must reap what the fathers have sown ?

Peace ! do you prate of peace when love is given in vain ?

When the slayer still goes forth and the women weep over the

slain ?

50

'Tis a peace more cruel than war, with a slanderous tongue

Killing swifter far than the deadliest shaft ever strung.

Peace ! do you prate of peace when the earth is sad to the
young ?

Peace ! when the poet's noblest words are those that are left
unsung ?

For this did Plato sing you Truth, that you so glibly lie ?

For this did Christ live you His life, and teach you His love—
and die ?

' Peace ! to appease an angry God ! And since He died,' you say,

' Peace reigns on earth, and Love, and all sins are washed away.'

Ha ! Pharisees, cast down your eyes where Peace is said to dwell,

And Love, and Truth, and Fellowship, and heaven on earth—or

hell !

Peace ! Oh, we scorn your peace ! 'Tis a cowardly blot which stains

The shield of a nation's honour, merely for money-market gains.

Peace ! you cry, for the workers must be crushed with an iron

hand,

That their lords may maintain their position and feed on the fat

of the land.

Peace ! when the press of the battle closes faster and faster around ?

Peace ! Let your impotent voices be lost in the glorious sound

Of the leaders calling the watchword, ' Men ! fight for the truth,
    and be free ;
For the braver the soldier, the sweeter his rest in the peace which
    shall be !

Peace ! 'Tis the peace of the angry breakers ere they fall ! '
Peace! 'Tis the pause of the soldiers 'twixt the charge and the
    clarion call !
Then the surge will thunder onward till it bursts on a boundless
    shore,
And the soldiers 'neath Freedom's banner must fight for the
    truth evermore !

A MOONLESS NIGHT

THERE is no moon to-night.

In love's despite,

Behind yon mist of grey

She's hidden away.

In heaven there is no light.

To-night I thought to dream

Within her silver beam ;

But the slow summer rain

Beats on the window-pane,
54

And the drip, drip of its stream

Beats in upon my brain,

Like water slowly hollowing a stone ;

    And the moon is gone !

No solitary star

Shines out afar ;

And in my soul no ray

Breaks, for my moon's away,

And the clouds my comrades are,

Heavy and drear and grey.

Drip, drip, their weary weeping still goes on ;

And my love has gone !

MEMORY'S LYRE

I LEANED my soul on memory's lyre,

    And touched, with tender tone,

The music of the bygone years,

The childish hopes, the maiden's fears,

Love's later dreams, with smiles and tears

    Of April all its own ;

But lingered longest on the strings

Which spoke of spirit wanderings.

The broken rack fled o'er the sky,

    A harbinger of storm ;

56

But wilder still my spirit, fraught

With hollow echoings of thought,

In dizzy undulations caught

    My unresisting form,

And swept me down its tide to dreams

Of death which is, is not, or seems.

My childish thought of that Beyond

    Humanity doth crave

Was ever marred by anguished pain,

And longing to behold again

The green mound, sodden with the rain

    Of one forsaken grave.

My fancy could not over-pass

The limits where I knew he was.

But later, when the shielding arms

    Were less missed than before,

And human nearness slipped away

To the drear cold of distant clay,

And the accustomed thought that day

    Would never see him more;

Then, through the darkness, dawning broke,

Divinest dreams of heaven awoke.

DO I LOVE THEE?

Do I love thee, my beloved?

More than the sea, which, unreproved,

Kisses the beauties of some balmy isle

Where, thro' full summer, splendid flowers smile;

And as the waves their yearning passion pour,

Drinking the spicy fragrance of that southern shore,

So would I love thee more and more,

So would I clasp thee o'er and o'er,

More than the sea !

59

Do I love thee, my beloved?

More than yon star, which, unremoved,

Its steadfast watch doth shining keep

When all the weary world's asleep,

And its clear light alone in heaven

To some sad wanderer is given!

As that pure spirit, from its airy car

So would I watch, so shine afar,

More than yon star!

LIFE

THERE dwells a spirit in the evening star,

Whom lovers' hearts look up to, lovers' sighs,

Filled with all happy dreams of hope, arise.

A spirit, too, there is, who, strong, doth keep

Watch o'er the wide and undulating deep ;

Who sends a mighty influence to bar

Its restless tides and lull its storms to sleep.

And there are spirits of the wandering breeze,

Who, with a faëry phantasy, enwreathe

61

The filmèd clouds, the winding mists ; who breathe,

To shiv'ring songsters, message that the Spring,

From far-off isles of heaven, is on the wing.

Spirits who gently wake to life the trees,

And o'er their boughs a greening mantle fling.

But One there is all other ones beside,

Who dwells not in the wind, nor in the storms ;

Who, ever formless, hath a thousand forms ;

Who, voiceless, bids a thousand hearts aspire ;

Who, torchless, sets a thousand hearts on fire ;

Who, deathless, yet a thousand times hath died ;

And highest, yet is yearning ever higher.

Life !   Star and spirit, deathless flame, 'tis thee,

In dwelling wonder, who hast mighty birth

Within the dust of man, light dust of earth !

Soul, down the endless ages wandering,

Who reachest, through those æons as they spring,

Unfathomed deeps of Immortality

On indestructible and tireless wing.

RAIN

The bents are brown

   In low'ring light,

   The mists roll white,

   The clouds are drifting,

   The winds are shifting,

And the smoke blows down.

Sudden the rain,

   With silver flail,

   Shining and pale,

With wild winds sweeping,

Wailing and weeping,

Drives over the plain.

LIMITATIONS

WOULD'ST thou enclose

Within thy hand a rose

  Of love without the thorn ?

Seek not to part

The shut doors of the heart

  In jest or scorn.

Press not too far

Thy hand within the jar,

  Lest the stored drops o'erflow.

66

Restrain thy haste

More than enough to taste.

   Take that, then go !

Things bought or sold

Are thine to take and hold—

   Thine at thy will ;

But man's deep heart

Is proffered in no mart,

   Unfettered still !

Stay, nor intrude,

Upon a spirit's mood

Unknown to thine.

Wait till the thought

Comes, blesses, speaks unsought

Revealed divine.

Then stand aside,

Not entering with pride,

Push and presume,

Deeming no worth,

In that thou tread'st to earth

An angel's plume.

Take it, confessed

A Heaven's gift, to thy breast

And, kneeling there,

Give thanks that blind,

Faithless, thou still can'st find

God everywhere.

SONG

THE skies are blue,

The day's begun ;

A sweet breeze, too—

The sweetest one.

The sun brings you—

Ah ! sweet the sun.

The clouds are grey,

The wild winds moan.

70

Ah ! dreary day,

The sunlight flown ;

And you away,

And I—alone !

MAY.

Ah! were it always May,

Haply light love would stay—

May, with her orchard snows,

May, when the blue-bell blows.

Ah! were it always May,

Haply light love would stay!

NOW!

Now, with your arms around me,

Now, when your kiss has crowned me,

Now, while your love has bound me

Fast, oh ! fast within the net

Bind and bind me faster yet.

Ah ! in this moment, all divine,

When life and soul are one with thine,

Since life's so sweet, sweet death would be

Thus clasped, thus kissed, thus loved by thee !

One moment more, and swift between
73

Our spirits would the mortal screen

With dreary distance intervene ;

And Now would go where Time encloses

All loveliest dreams with last year's roses

Deep in some fragrant buried store,

Where we could reach it nevermore.

We, parted from this close embrace,

Should strive in vain this hour to trace

In distant light of other days.

Nay, Fate shall never have its will ;

Now, while you love me, love me still.

One last long kiss on lips, on brow !

Oh ! perfect bliss !   Come death, come—now !

AN ARABIAN LOVE SONG

In passionate shimmer of a full moon-rise

He came. Ah! then were looks from liquid eyes,

And close embrace, and love's low-breathëd sighs.

Then silence, as if each one feared to break

Some sweet dream's spell, and lonely still, awake.

Through dewy airs the languid perfumes float,

Drawn from rich flowers, while the bulbul's note

Throbs out such music from its swelling throat

That earth, and air, and starry heaven above

Seem but one melody—and that is love !

AVE ATQUE VALE

No last appeal from your soul unto mine.

I cannot let you go, and make no sign.

The light sinks dim—light which seemed half-divine,

So thrilled it was with heaven, when it used to shine

Through deep June eventides dead long ago.

Ah ! my beloved, I cannot let you go.

On some June night, when slumber leaves your brow,

Will no sad thoughts arise of Junes we used to know—

Thoughts of the silvered stream, the pallid moon hung low,

And we two drifting with the river's flow?

Oh! my beloved, in no wandering

Will thy soul stoop with mine to drink of Love's well-spring?

No last appeal?   Well, that old dream is o'er.

Go!   Live thy happy life, love as you loved before,

Murm'ring to other ears the well-remembered lore;

I claim no jot of all that love you bore.

But stay!   One place is mine within your memory;

For when you think of June, you think of me!

That place is mine; and 'neath the river's wave,

While you and Love float on, perchance a grave.